To LEE
with much love
from Uncle Brian
& Auntie Jannette
x x (4/10/87)

for
Tremayne
and
Piers

Angry Arthur

Text by Hiawyn Oram
Pictures by Satoshi Kitamura

PUFFIN BOOKS

Once there was a boy called Arthur.
He wanted to stay up and watch
the western on T.V.

"No," said his mother,
"it's too late. Go to bed."
"I'll get angry," said Arthur.
"Get angry,"
said his mother.

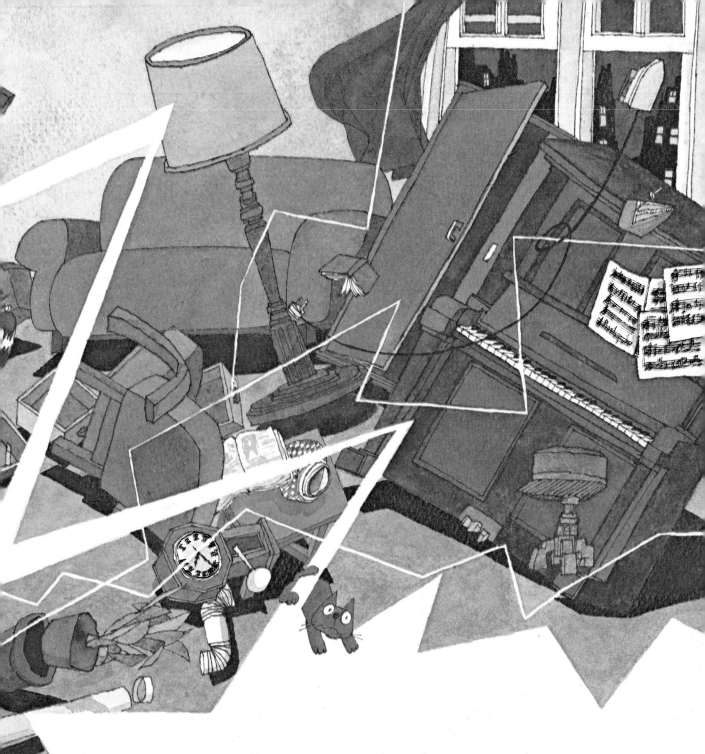

So he did. Very, very angry.
He got so angry that his anger became a stormcloud
exploding thunder and lightning and hailstones.

"That's enough,"
said his mother.
But it wasn't.

Arthur's anger became a hurricane hurling rooftops
and chimneys and church spires.

"That's enough,"
said his father.
But it wasn't.

Arthur's anger became a typhoon
tipping whole towns
into the seas.

"That's enough," said his grandfather.
But it wasn't.

Arthur's anger became an earth tremor cracking the
surface of the earth like a giant cracking eggs.
"That's enough," said his grandmother.
But it wasn't.

Arthur's anger became a universequake

and the earth and the moon

and the stars and the planets,

Arthur's country and Arthur's town, his street,
his house, his garden and his bedroom

were nothing more
than bits in space.

Arthur sat on a piece of Mars and thought.
He thought and thought.

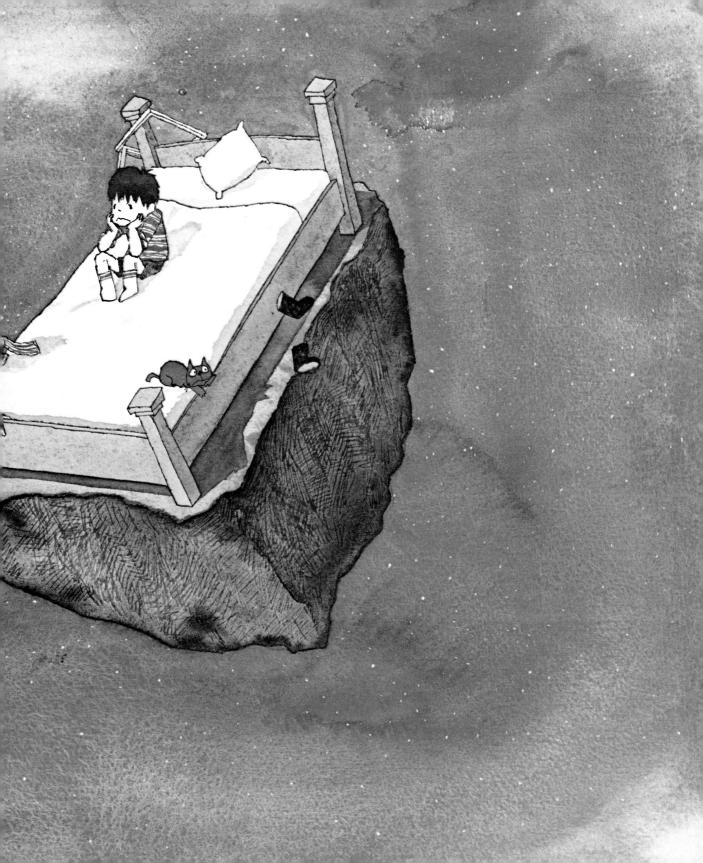

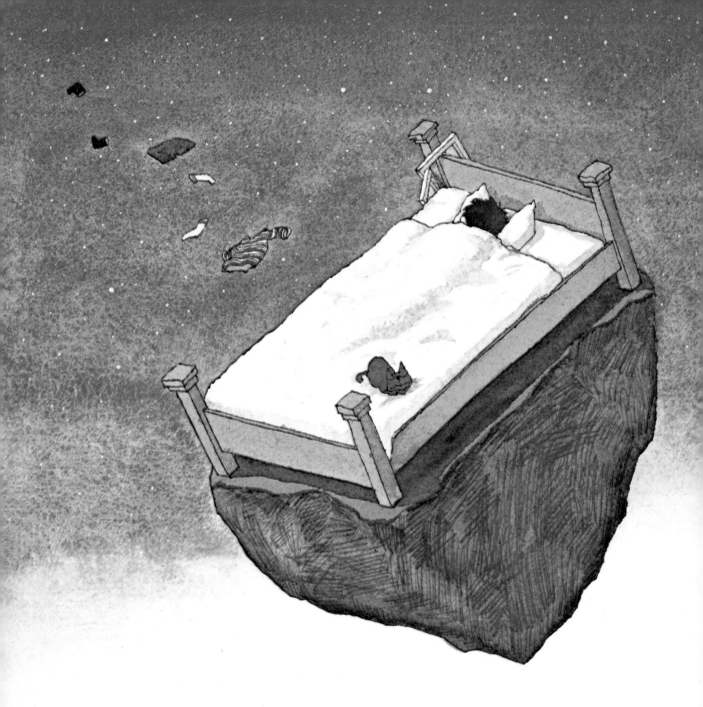

"Why was I so angry?" he thought.
He never did remember.
Can you?